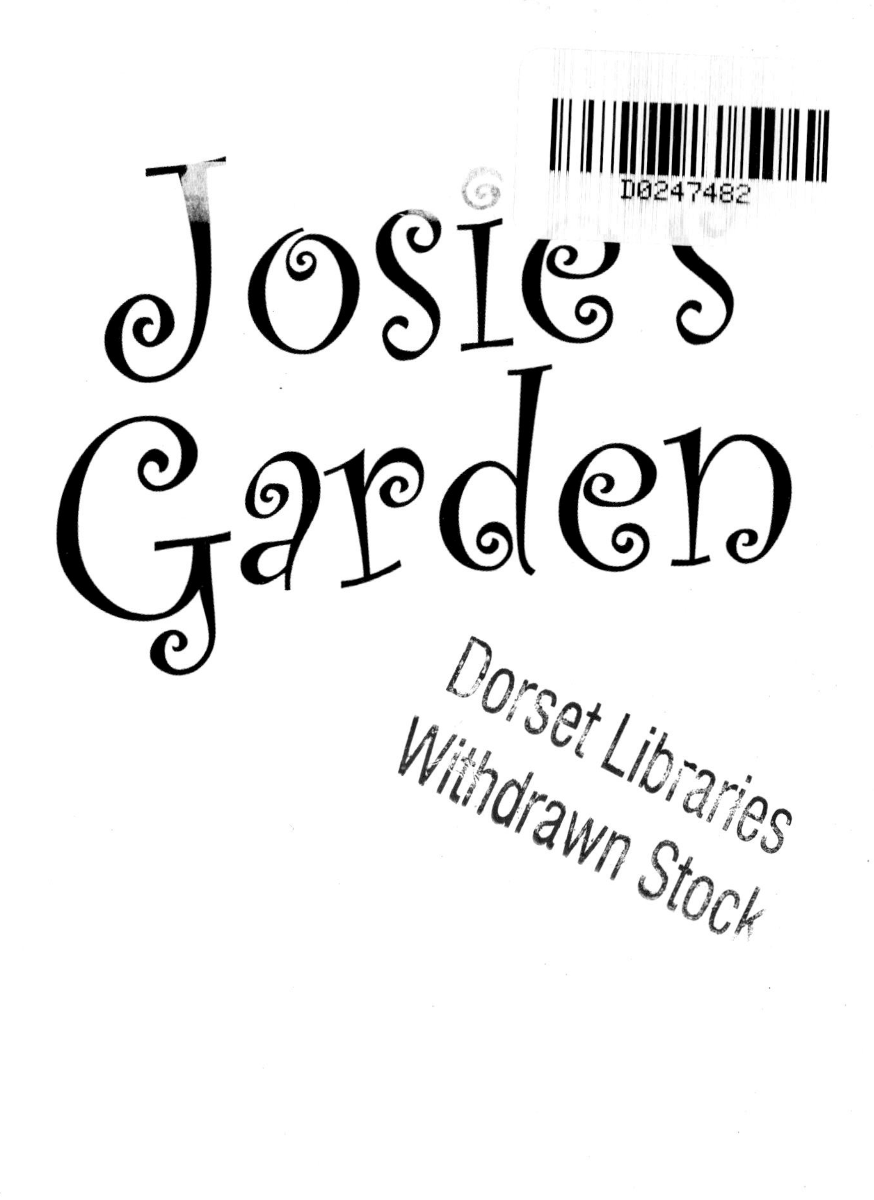

Josie's Garden

Josie's Garden

by David Orme
and Martin Remphry

First published 2009 by
Evans Brothers Limited
2A Portman Mansions
Chiltern St
London W1U 6NR

Orme, David
Josie's garden. – (Skylarks)
1. Children's stories.
I. Title II. Series
823.9'14-dc22

ISBN: HB 978 0 237 53906 1
ISBN: PB 978 0 237 53893 4

Printed in China by New Era Printing Co. Ltd

Series Editor: Louise John
Design: Robert Walster
Production: Jenny Mulvanny

Contents

Chapter One

Josie Granger was feeling grumpy. It was Sunday afternoon and Josie wanted to go out, but Mum wouldn't let her. Mum ran her own business from home, making curtains and cushions, and she usually took Josie out on Sundays, but today she had a special order to get ready for Monday morning.

"You know you can't go out by yourself," Mum said. "And I'm sorry, but I'm just too busy to take you. I don't like having to work on a Sunday either, but we need the money. Why don't you see what's on television?"

"I don't want to," Josie grumbled. "Why can't we move to a house with a garden? Then I could play outside and still be safe."

Mum, Josie and her brother, Henry, lived in a flat, high up in a tower block in the middle of town. It was great living there, because you could see right across the town to the hills, and watch all the people and traffic scurrying about below.

It was a lovely flat – but it didn't have a garden.

Josie picked up her reading book, but she didn't really want to read. Mum was struggling with a great length of red velvet. She had pins sticking out of her mouth.

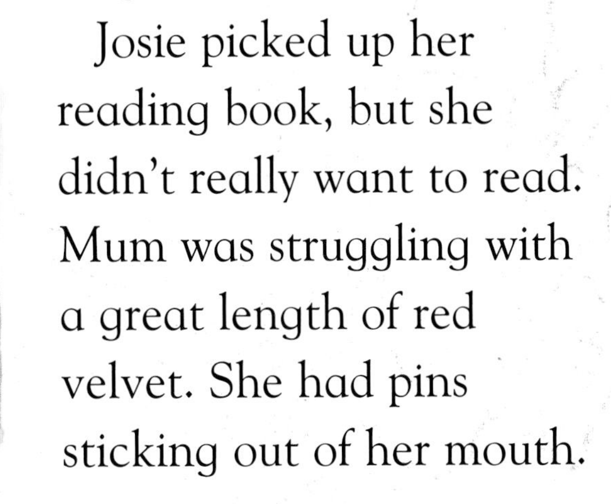

"Maybe you'll earn enough money one day to buy a house with a garden, and I can grow all sorts of things and have lots of wild animals to look after," said Josie.

Mum laughed. "Maybe," she said and gave Josie a big hug.

Chapter Two

Just then, the doorbell rang. It was Stuart's dad bringing Henry home from Stuart's birthday party. Henry bustled into the living room.

"I suppose it's teatime," said Mum. "Mind you don't tread on those curtains with your dirty feet, Henry."

She went off into the kitchen to make the tea and Henry turned the television on.

"I don't imagine you want anything to eat, Henry," called Mum. "Not after a birthday tea."

"We only had burgers and sausages and chips and cake," said Henry. "I'm still starving!"

That night Josie lay in bed, half asleep. The sound of Mum's sewing machine hummed and rattled away in the next room. She was thinking about her garden, and the sound of the sewing machine turned into the humming of bees, visiting tall pink flowers.

"Maybe one day soon," she thought, just before she fell asleep. "I'll have a garden all of my own..."

Chapter Three

The sun was shining as Josie and Henry left for school the next day. Mum took them as far as the lollipop man, Mr Carter. Henry met Stuart and some of their friends and went rushing off with them.

Josie dawdled along with her friend,

Meena. Meena had a very tiny garden and Josie sometimes went round to play. It had tall buildings all around it and the sun didn't reach it very often, so the flowers that Meena's mother tried to grow were weak and straggly.

Next door to the school was an old church, boarded up and sad-looking. A long shoot covered in purple flowers hung over the tall fence that separated the two buildings. A brightly-coloured butterfly rested on the shoot, its wings stretched out in the sun.

"Look!" said Josie. "There must be a garden behind that fence."

"There is," said Meena. "There's a big gap in the fence just round the corner and you can see in."

The old churchyard had become a

wild and overgrown garden. Small trees pushed their way up through nettles and docks, and tall pink flowers swayed in the bright sunlight. A great bush hung over the fence and butterflies rested on its purple flowers. Near the church wall were some beautiful golden flowers. Ivy scrambled up the wall and sparrows flew in and out of it.

"It's a magic garden!" said Josie excitedly. "I want to explore it!"

"Well, we can't," said Meena. "It's time for school. Anyway, it might not be safe."

"Of course it's safe," said Josie. "I'm going to explore it on the way home. And you're coming too!"

Chapter Four

All that day at school Josie thought of nothing but the garden. At home time she met Meena and Ben in the playground. Ben was another of Josie's friends and she had told him about the garden. They were going to explore!

Even though there was a noisy road

outside, the garden seemed a quiet place. The butterflies still fluttered around the big bush. A blackbird watched them from a pile of bent iron and concrete. Pigeons came and went through a broken window high up in the church. White seeds floated like stars from the tall flowers.

Meena wasn't thinking about flowers. "I've just trodden in something smelly," she grumbled.

Ben looked down. "A hedgehog did that," he said. "I know because my auntie's garden has got hedgehogs in it."

Josie was excited. "Let's wait a bit longer. We might see a hedgehog!"

Meena wiped her shoe on the grass. "Hedgehogs only come out at night, silly. Anyway, it's time to go. Our mums will be waiting for us at the crossing."

They climbed back through the hole in the fence and hurried along to Mr Carter. Josie had never seen a hedgehog before. Somehow or other, she was going to make sure she saw one before long!

Chapter Five

Mum was waiting by the crossing with Henry. Meena's father came hurrying along. He waved when he saw Meena.

"I'm glad you were a bit late today. I'm late too!" he said. Mr Begum was always busy. He was a governor of the school and a local councillor. People went to see him when they had problems with their houses or when their bins didn't get emptied. "I'll see what I can do," he would say.

Henry was in a mood. "Where have you been?" he grumbled. "You know my programme starts at four o'clock!" He set off grumpily towards home. Mum and Josie followed behind.

Josie didn't tell Mum about the garden. She wanted to keep it as her own special secret.

After tea, Stuart came round to see if Henry was allowed out. He had two other friends with him from school. Mum didn't like them playing in the streets, but she said it would be all right as long as they were back before seven o'clock.

Josie had brought a book home from the school library about wild flowers and trees. Mum had no curtains to do so she sat and watched television. Josie curled up next to her with the book, trying to work out the names of the flowers in the garden. She found the tall pink flower straight away. It had two names. One was rosebay willowherb and the other was fireweed. She liked fireweed best.

The big golden flowers were called golden rod. She couldn't find the big bushy plant with the purple flowers, so she gave it a name of her own – the butterfly bush.

Henry was looking pleased with himself when he got home.

"We've had a great time!" he said. "We're building a gang hut. We've found a brilliant place by the school. There's some old sheets of metal and some planks, and some trees we can chop down, too. It's only an old dump, and nobody else wants it. We've started work already chopping down nettles and things!"

Chapter Six

Neither Henry nor Mum expected what happened next. Josie shot off the sofa, burst into tears, and leapt on Henry, thumping him with her fists.

"That's my place!" she shouted between sobs. "That's my secret! You can't have it, you can't, you can't!"

Mum grabbed her and pulled her off.

"Josie! Whatever is the matter with you? I'm fed up with you two fighting all the time. Henry hasn't done anything wrong! Go to your room!"

Still sobbing, Josie went to her room. Outside, the traffic rumbled along far below, past her garden. *Her* garden. What had Henry and his friends done to it? She had to know!

Very quietly she slipped on her outdoor shoes and went into the hall. The television chattered away in the living room. She put on her coat and opened the front door, carefully shutting it behind her so that no one would hear it bang.

Chapter Seven

The streets were still busy as Josie hurried towards the garden. All the shops selling food were open for business, and she could smell the different flavours as she hurried along – fish and chips, curry and Chinese food. She soon reached the busy road where

Mr Carter waited to see them across. Of course, Mr Carter wasn't there now, but when the road was clear, Josie walked over. The big fence with the posters came next. She went round the corner and slipped through the hole in the fence.

At first, the garden looked the same. Sparrows chattered in the ivy, and the fireweed seeds drifted off in the late evening sunshine. Then Josie saw Henry's hut, an ugly pile of planks propped up with bricks. A piece of wavy iron was fixed over the top.

The boys hadn't chopped down any of the flowers, but the area round the hut had been trampled flat and was bare and brown. The planks and iron had been dragged along the ground, and all the creatures that lived beneath them had rushed off, to find other dark places before the birds spotted them.

Josie was too angry to cry. Henry would soon start chopping down the flowers and trees. He wouldn't let Josie come to the garden anymore. She knew that Henry hadn't really meant to do any harm. It was just that he didn't understand about wild things.

Josie wanted the ugly old hut to go, now. She gave a great tug at the roof.

The whole hut rocked. She gave another huge heave and the hut crashed down. A heavy plank of wood twisted round and fell against Josie's leg. She felt a terrible pain where it hit her and she screamed. The pain wouldn't go away. She found herself lying in the long grass and dock leaves, and the pain was so terrible she couldn't cry out any more.

Josie thought she must have gone to sleep for a while. When she came to, it was getting dark. A faint scrabbling noise must have woken her. The pain wasn't so terrible now, as long as she didn't move. Out from a clump of nettles came a busy hedgehog. He took no notice of Josie. She lay still and quiet, watching him trotting across the garden, sniffing out a tasty supper of slugs and earthworms. Josie watched until he disappeared from her view, then twisted round so that she could see what he was going to do next.

When she moved the dreadful pain in her leg came back. She screamed out. A voice called out over the fence.

"Is there anyone there? Is someone in trouble?"

Josie cried out again. "Help me! Please!"

A worried-looking face poked through the hole in the fence. It was Meena's father!

Mr Begum was quite large round the middle, and it was a squeeze to get through the hole in the fence.

"Why, you're Meena's little friend!" he said in astonishment. "What has happened to you? Whatever are you doing here?"

Chapter Eight

Josie quite enjoyed the hospital. Everybody made a fuss of her, and she had lots of visitors. She couldn't remember very much about the night the accident had happened. There had been a blue flashing light, and kind hands that had lifted her into an ambulance, and Mr Begum, who had held her hand on the way to the hospital. Then Mum had arrived, and Josie remembered she had been crying. Josie had gone to sleep and had woken up in a big bed with crispy sheets. Her leg felt funny and, when she felt it, she found it was covered in plaster.

"A nasty break," the doctor had said. "But it'll be as good as new soon."

Mr Begum had been to see her, and so had Mrs Sherret, the headteacher. She told both of them about the garden and about not having a garden of her own and how she didn't want Henry and his friends to spoil it. Mr Begum scratched his head and said, "I'll see what I can do." Just the way he always did.

Henry had come too. He said he was very sorry about what had happened and he didn't know it had been Josie's special place.

After a few days, Josie went home. She was able to walk around now with some crutches, but she was told not to overdo it. She nagged and nagged Mum to take her to see the garden.

"It'll be autumn soon and all the flowers will die before I can see them," she said. But Mum wouldn't take her.

After a week Josie visited the hospital again and the doctor said that Josie could go back to school. She was desperate to see her garden again.

Mr Begum came round to take Josie in his car, as it was too far for her to walk on her crutches. She swept past Mr

Carter feeling very grand. She looked towards the garden – and the fence was gone!

Mr Begum stopped the car and helped Josie and her mum out. The whole school seemed to be waiting on the pavement for her! With the fence gone, the garden seemed changed. The trees were still there, and the wild flowers, but most of the rubbish had gone.

There was a hole in the ground with a plastic sheet inside. On the wall of the church was a big notice:

Everybody cheered like mad when they saw Josie, and Mrs Sherret came forward and took her into the garden. She explained that when the church had closed down the council had taken over the piece of land.

When Mr Begum had heard Josie's story in the hospital, he persuaded the council to give the garden to the school, to celebrate a very important date – the school was a hundred years old that year! Mrs Sherret and the top class had started work straight away. The hole was to be a pond, so that frogs could breed and the hedgehog would have somewhere close by to drink.

Josie was thrilled but there was just one small thing bothering her.

"Why did you cut down the butterfly

bush?" she said.

Mrs Sherret smiled. "It will grow again next year and be even stronger, now we have cut it back," she said. "Even wild gardens need to be looked after. So hurry up and get better. We're going to need as much help with this one as we can get!"

If you enjoyed this story, why not read another *Skylarks* book?

The Emperor's New Clothes
by Louise John and Serena Curmi

There once lived an emperor who was proud and vain and spent all his money on clothes. One day, two scoundrels arrived at the palace and persuaded the emperor that they could weave magical cloth. He set them to work making him a fine set of robes. But the emperor had a lesson to learn, and his new clothes were quite a sight to behold!

The Lion and the Gypsy
by Jillian Powell and Heather Deen

Fatima the wandering gypsy is tired and lies down to sleep. A sand-coloured lion roams through the desert. He is hungry and looking for tasty morsels to eat. He stops and sniffs the air, and the scent of a human reaches his nose. He follows the footprints and, on silent paws, he creeps around the sleeping gypsy, sniffing hungrily. Fatima has no idea of the danger she is in...

Merbaby

by Penny Kendal and Claudia Venturini

One day at the beach, Anna, Ellie and Joe find a funny-looking fish in a rock pool. To their surprise, they find that the fish is a baby mermaid! They take the merbaby home in a bucket and keep it a secret from Mum. But, four-year-old Joe isn't very good at keeping secrets, and soon the merbaby is in danger. Will Anna and Ellie be able to save her?

Noah's Shark

by Alan Durant and Holly Surplice

Noah was fed up with the people in his world making a right mess of everything. He built a big boat to escape in, and invited his animal friends along – couples only! The animals queued up by the boat, two by two. All except for Mrs Shark, who came alone. It seemed she had accidentally eaten her husband! Would Noah be able to trust her on his boat?

Skylarks titles include:

Awkward Annie
by Julia Williams and Tim Archbold
HB 9780237533847 / PB 9780237534028

Sleeping Beauty
by Louise John and Natascia Ugliano
HB 9780237533861 / PB 9780237534042

Detective Derek
by Karen Wallace and Beccy Blake
HB 9780237533885 / PB 9780237534066

Hurricane Season
by David Orme and Doreen Lang
HB 9780237533892 / PB 9780237534073

Spiggy Red
by Penny Dolan and Cinzia Battistel
HB 9780237533854 / PB 9780237534035

London's Burning
by Pauline Francis and Alessandro Baldanzi
HB 9780237533878 / PB 9780237534059

The Black Knight
by Mick Gowar and Graham Howells
HB 9780237535803 / PB 9780237535926

Ghost Mouse
by Karen Wallace and Beccy Blake
HB 9780237535827 / PB 9780237535940

Yasmin's Parcels
by Jill Atkins and Lauren Tobia
HB 9780237535858 / PB 9780237535971

Muffin
by Anne Rooney and Sean Julian
HB 9780237535810 / PB 9780237535933

Tallulah and the Tea Leaves
by Louise John and Vian Oelofsen
HB 9780237535841 / PB 9780237535964

The Big Purple Wonderbook
by Enid Richemont and Helen Jackson
HB 9780237535834 / PB 9780237535957

Noah's Shark
by Alan Durant and Holly Surplice
HB 9780237539047 / PB 9780237538910

The Emperor's New Clothes
by Louise John and Serena Curmi
HB 9780237539085 / PB 9780237538958

Carving the Sea Path
by Kathryn White and Evelyn Duverne
HB 9780237539030 / PB 9780237538903

Merbaby
by Penny Kendal and Claudia Venturini
HB 9780237539078 / PB 9780237538941

The Lion and the Gypsy
by Jillian Powell and Heather Deen
HB 9780237539054 / PB 9780237538927

Josie's Garden
by David Orme and Martin Remphry
HB 9780237539061 / PB 9780237538934